The Seventh Whistleblower

by

Dr. Monica Handy

Books by M. Handy

A subdivision of *COOTW* Literary Works

Copyright © 2022 by Monica Handy

All rights reserved.

ISBN: 978-1-7368777-1-5

Printed in the United States of America

First Printing: June 2025

COOTW LITERARY WORKS

Dedication

For the ones who see too much and say too little, the Whistleblower is here.

Acknowledgments

This book wouldn't exist without the people who stood quietly in the margins, urging me on.

Thank you to my family, friends, and peers for your support, insights, and patience.

To my readers—especially those who've ever felt unheard or unseen—thank you for trusting me with your time. I hope this story finds you where you are and leaves you a little stronger than you were before.

About the Author

Monica Handy is a creative writer, with a passion for uncovering the truths hidden in plain sight.

When not writing, she can be found drinking coffee and questioning details. The Seventh Whistleblower is her latest novel.

Chapter 1

The Snub

Claire's heart pounded in her ears as she faced Sam—merciless, sharp-tongued, and known throughout Brunston as Sling Blade.

Beads of sweat formed along her brow as nerves gripped the pit of her stomach. The silence in the room seemed to close in. Her only comfort was what she held in her hands—the result of months of research and sleepless nights, a presentation painstakingly crafted, every word measured, deliberate, exact.

Still, a flicker of insecurity—and even flashes of rage—flared in her chest at the thought of being judged. Sam rarely saw her work as little more than fodder for critique.

Beside her, Kat, her best friend since grammar school, stood with the other critics, arms crossed, and lips curved in a faint smirk. Claire's stomach twisted. Kat knew exactly how much was on the line with this assignment. Yet here she was, siding with Sam's gaze rather than offering the support Claire so desperately needed.

What do you mean, 'an improvement'?" came her shaky reply into the tense silence.

Sam paused mid–forkful of salad—Ranch dressing dripping from his sausage-like finger. He chewed slowly, eyes narrowing. "These are excellent myths," he said at last, "and perfect for a documentary—if everyone mentioned were deceased. But they're alive, major donors to our department, including Carla Burton. You're essentially saying these people of color haven't been honored—and slapping it on..." He flipped her title page with a sneer... "Bridging the Racial Divide."

Claire's cheeks burned. "Every bit of that story is fact! It's all true!"

"You get an A for assumption," Sam continued, voice low. "But the world's tired of conspiracy theories, 'blacks suffering, and tabloid sex scandals. Who gives a—?" He paused, lips curling.

Claire's chest tightened. Sweat ran down her temple. She pressed her palms flat on the table. "I do."

Sam set down his fork. The clock ticked—slow and merciless. He leaned forward, wiping his greasy fingers on a napkin with deliberate slowness.

"Look, you're not wrong for caring. But caring doesn't pass final exams, sell newspapers, or pay bills. You wanna make headlines, Ida B. Wells—you wanna ignite change? Then do it without dragging our donors into a PR nightmare." He locked eyes with her. "You have three days to pull this off. Find another angle—or fail."

"Fail?!" she shot back, her voice sharper than intended. Claire had never raised her voice to a superior before. The room held its breath.

"That's right," Sam said. "Fail. Journalism isn't for the faint of heart."

The word, "Fail" rang in her ears, but it wasn't just Sam's ultimatum that shook her—it was Kat's silence. Claire looked toward her, hoping for the old ally to reemerge, the one who believed in her no matter what.

They'd walked home from grammar school every afternoon, sacred secrets and Nancy Drew dreams tumbling between them. They pooled nickels to split candy bars "even-Steven," convinced betrayal was unthinkable. They swore never to turn on each other, even if the whole world did. Back then, loyalty flowed freely—effortlessly. Not anymore.

Chapter 2

Day 1

The long walk to the campus café did little to ease Claire's worry. Sam's deadline loomed like a guillotine, impossible to meet. But failure? Not an option. Worse than the timeline were his comments dismissing her pitch as "dated." As if discrimination came with an expiration date. She shook her head. Maybe all rich white boys from the Hamptons had lost their damn minds.

The cashier cleared her throat, directing Claire's gaze to the overhead menu. She ordered a clove and pineapple tea and tucked herself into a corner booth near a window. She needed to breathe, recalibrate, and cling to her convictions. The scent of spiced tea helped her center, and her shoulders began to loosen. Outside, students drifted along the garden path, their carefree pace a stark contrast to the storm brewing in her life.. Slowly, her thoughts began to shift and settle on the details in her pitch to Sam.

Fact one: Blush, North Dakota, was overwhelmingly white and home to Brunston University, one of the most elite journalism schools in the country. Fact two: The administration was politely hostile toward Affirmative Action, preferring to brag about not handing out "free rides" while forever throwing fundraisers that masqueraded as galas. Red flag much? Fact three: Some of the biggest names in Prime-Time Broadcasting were Brunston alums—and if rumors were true, not all of them earned their degrees under equal conditions.

Carla Burton, Channel 6's star anchor, was among them. A striking woman of color, Carla came from old California wine money—her parents, Carl and Mattie Burton, were powerhouse defense attorneys. Carla graduated summa cum laude, Brunston's first Black woman to do so. It should have been a straightforward triumph. But in journalism, nothing is ever that simple.

Claire took a long sip of her tea. The story she'd built, full of facts but devoid of fire, wasn't enough. She sighed. Sam was right—this wasn't the story for this town. No one in Blush wanted to read about the accomplishments of people they preferred not to think about. Claire realized she'd played it too safe. But now? She was finally on fire.

She bolted from the café and raced across the quad, her bag bouncing against her hip. At the library, she made a mad dash to the media room and cut off a fellow student to claim the last cubicle.

"Hey! We don't do that here!" he snapped.

Too late. Claire was already deep in the university archives. The public records documented Carla's academic accolades in crisp detail—but gave almost nothing away about her personal life. So, Claire went deeper, following the breadcrumbs to those around her. That's when she found it: a thirty-year-old newspaper article featuring Carla's father.

In the mid-seventies, a small Los Angeles publication covered a civil lawsuit filed against a prestigious Midwestern university—Carl Burton had served as lead attorney. Seven inner-
city scholarship students, four Black, one Native American, one Latino, and one unnamed plaintiff, had taken the institution to court.

Claire frowned. Who was the anonymous seventh student—and why the secrecy?

The article described substandard dorm conditions: crumbling infrastructure, vermin, and faulty wiring. Meal cards that offered them only salads and shrink-wrapped sandwiches while other students enjoyed full buffets. Same schedules, same coursework—but they were barred from the gym, study groups, and libraries. Isolated in their deteriorating dorm, they talked. And the more they talked, the more they realized they were being systematically shut out. They decided to raise their voices. The university appeared to address their complaints by patching things with subpar materials. Until one day, it wasn't enough.

Claire sat back, breath caught. This wasn't just a story. It was the beginning of an investigation.

Chapter 3

Everybody is So Hush-Hush

After the thousandth patch job on the electrical wiring and plunging toilets until their arms ached, Valentina and Bala began to crack. None of the others knew how much until Bala had a meltdown in the library while trying to check out The Five Ws of Journalism, and Valentina went behind the lunch counter to prepare herself some roast beef and potatoes.

The revolution had begun—but was swiftly met with disciplinary action. Both were placed on three-month probation, and Valentina's dining privileges were revoked.

Claire, still engrossed in her research on the 1978 Whistleblower case, felt the injustice echoing across time. She shook her head at the obvious mistreatment of those students and fought to control her emotions. Surely Carla Burton had been aware of the case—her father had defended the plaintiffs, and their timelines on campus overlapped. Claire was so absorbed in the story that she barely noticed the man beside her standing to leave. Almost immediately, someone else slid into the vacant seat. When she looked up, it was Kat.

"Oh my goodness—not today, Kat!"

"Get over yourself, Claire."

"That's your suggestion? That I get over myself? Are you serious?! You're supposed to be my friend. You, of all people, know how hard I'm trying and how hard it is for me to fit in!"

"Maybe you should stop flaunting your Blackness."

"What does that even mean?!"

"Your afro-puffs, cornrows, and hula-hoop earrings, for one.

And let's not forget your Jesse Jackson and Barack Obama posters!"

"I never saw you as the shallow type, Kat. Have you drunk the Kool-Aid?!"

"No, not Kool-Aid—truth serum. In this world, you gotta fit in to make it. Our parents did it, and they're successful. You may want to ruin this opportunity with all your Black Pride, but you're not gonna ruin my future."

Claire shook her head again, this time in disgust.

"What happened to you? One minute we're walking home from grammar school, two little Black girls with dreams, and the next, I'm ruining your future?"

"I was always just a girl, Claire. Not a *Black* girl."

"Kat, that's quite a self-assessment. But for the record, straightening your hair and trying to Pilates your ass off doesn't cause fusion with this culture or any other. In my estimation, you did, in fact, drink the Kool-Aid of falsehood—which I'm forced to respect wholeheartedly. Now, run along with your colorless friends. I have work to do."

With that, she turned back to her computer as Kat stormed away.

Her fingers resumed moving feverishly over the keyboard, digging deeper for information about Carla Burton and the Whistleblowers. The results revealed redacted documents, leading her to believe the case had been settled out of court. There were, no doubt, gag orders in place as well. This was where the trail went cold.

Switching back to previous screens, she noted that as a freshman, Carla appeared confident and stylish standing beside her white peers. But as time went on, her appearance became less maintained—even haggard. Maybe it was the heavy class load. Because the light was gone.

From there, Claire made a list of the plaintiffs' names, instinctively feeling like Bala Agarwal had guts and a story to tell. It was 6 p.m., and that would be it for the day. Tired and hungry, she decided to make her way to the dining hall before it closed. With each step, Claire felt the weight and shame of those seven students. It was heavy and degrading.

The woman who rang up her dinner was an older Mexican woman who may have been around long enough to remember something.

"Please slide your dinner card through the machine, precioso."

The woman had called her *precious*-Claire smiled as she slid her card through the machine.

"Señorita. I'm writing a documentary for my Journalism class and was wondering if you know anything about the old dormitories-from back in the late seventies?"

"You're the second one this month asking about that place. I'll tell you the same thing—very dangerous, Chica! Those things were closed down years ago after a tragedy occurred. My advice: stay away."

Tragedy? The word echoed. Now Claire had every intention of digging deeper.

"Someone else came by asking about the old dorms?"

"Sí. The man in the journalism department. He always orders Chef Salad with plenty of extra ranch dressing."

"Sam?!"

"Sí! Señor Sam! That is him."

"Gracias, Señorita. One more thing—what tragedy?" Claire asked, trying to sound casual.

"I don't have time to talk. My cousin Jimmy worked here during that time—go ask him," she said, pointing to a door just off the kitchen.

Approaching the open door of a small office, Claire knocked, rousing an older Mexican man from menu planning.

"Yes, may I help you?"

"Yes, sir. I'm working on a documentary about a trailblazing woman of color who graduated from Brunston in '79. I'm hoping to speak with people who know her personally."

"Who is this woman?"

"Carla Burton," Claire said with a smile.

The old man slowly looked up from his computer and made eye contact. His thick gray brows arched in a way that said he was deeply disturbed.

"I'd also like to take some photos of her old dorm room. You know, a then-and-now thing."

"Leave it alone and get out of my office."
"Excuse me?"

"Have a good day," Jimmy said, shewing her toward the door.

"Señor, please. Tell me the location of those dorms."

Now he was standing for emphasis. "Every three years or so, some undergrad comes in asking about Carla Burton's life here on campus. For what I hope is the last time, the staff is prohibited from discussing her past. It's a privacy issue. Her records are sealed."

"Not according to the school archives."

"I'm talking personal files. You look a little bit like Carla, with the same dreams in your eyes. I can tell you now, no one at this college wants to answer questions about Carla Burton. Just get your degree and move forward."

There was a finality in his voice that demanded she leave. And that's what she did. At least Jimmy and the cashier confirmed her suspicions that something was wrong. They also added to her list of facts:

- Something terrible happened here at Brunston and it was connected to Carla Burton.

- There were personal, sealed documents from the late seventies that still frightened Jimmy.

- The old dorms that housed those seven students had not been condemned.

And last, but not least, what exactly was Sam's interest in this matter?

Chapter 4

Day 2

After a restless night filled with unanswered questions, Claire buried herself in internet searches for Bala Agarwal. Who knew there could be so many people with the same name? After narrowing her search by age, location, and education, Claire finally struck gold: a business profile showing father and son in matching blue shirts, captioned "Agarwal Broadcasting — The News of Our Nation." If that wasn't confirmation enough, two framed journalism degrees from Brunston University hung in the background. It was a small victory she celebrated with an hour of sleep.

Between classes, Claire called the Oklahoma-based news station again and again until someone finally picked up.

"You've reached Agarwal Broadcasting—The News of Our Nation. How may I direct your call?" said a woman with a nasal tone.

"I'd like to speak with Dr. Bala Agarwal Senior," Claire said, in her most professional voice.

"I'm sorry, the station owner isn't available at the moment. May I ask, what is the nature of this call?"

"I'm working on a documentary about Brunston alumni and came across Dr. Agarwal's name."

"May I take your name and number?"

"Sure."

I'll make sure he gets the message. Have a nice day."

And just like that, Claire was playing the waiting game. The only way to win was to stay busy—or sleep. She chose the latter, retreating to her dorm room for a nap.

Several hours later, a cool evening breeze stirred her awake. Disoriented, she blinked at the open window—had she opened it? She checked her phone. No missed calls. Disappointed, she dragged herself from bed to close the window.

That's when she saw it: a manila envelope on the floor, right in the middle of the room. Had someone slipped it in while she slept?

She examined the package—no return address. Just a manila envelope, plain and unmarked. Inside was a hand-drawn map and what looked like a padlock combination scrawled in the corner.

A chill ran down her spine. How had this even gotten here?

She wished Kay were with her—to squeal over the mystery, then shush each other with nervous laughter. But she was alone now. And it was far too late to back out.

She laid the map on the kitchen counter and leaned in, tracing each line carefully.

A particularly thick crooked line, snaked across the page, mapping what looked like a makeshift trail. One end pointed to a structure with a clock face—clearly the campus library. The other curved toward crude green triangles labeled as the Cottonwood grove. But it was the boxy symbol just beyond the trees that stopped her cold. No marked paths. Just woods.

At the bottom of the page were a string of letters and numbers she couldn't decipher. She needed help.

Bobby Johnson was the obvious choice. Numbers were his thing—he was a meteorology major, after all. The problem? Their last encounter had been... complicated.

Still, before she could overthink it, she found herself standing in the campus gym, directly in front of him as he did arm curls with his friends.

"Hey, Bobby!" she called out—too loudly.

He looked up and just stared.

"I was wondering if I could talk to you for a minute?"

His smirk said everything. "Look who decided I'm worth talking to now—Ms. 'Black is Beautiful.' Change your mind?"

"Look, I'm sorry about all that," she lied. "I'd just broken up with my boyfriend."

The truth was, Bobby was all about Bobby—and she hadn't wanted to be another notch on his belt. But right now, she needed his help.

"I need your help."

Despite himself, he looked intrigued.

"I'm listening."

Claire pulled the map from her pocket and pointed to the numbers. "What do these mean?"

He glanced at them. "Coordinates," he said casually, pulling out his phone and typing them in. "According to this, you've got something hidden about four miles into the Cottonwood grove. Whatever this is—sits just east of the clearing."

"There's a clearing?"

"From what I can tell."

"Thanks so much!" Claire said sincerely.

As she turned to leave, Bobby called after her. "What's this all about, Nancy Drew?"

She paused, then met his eyes. "Take a walk with me," she said, already turning toward the grove.

Chapter 5

The Old Dorm

"So, let me get this straight," Bobby said. "Your Journalism Professor thinks the achievements of African Americans are old news?"

"Pretty much. He said people are tired of hearing about conspiracies and Black suffering."

"Are you serious?!" he exploded.

"Calm down. I already made a fool of myself in front of the entire journalism department. That's why I'm in this mess."

"So now you have to rework your angle and pitch it again?!"

"You're kinda smart for a weatherman," she replied, deadpan. "The deadline's tomorrow. If I miss it, I fail the course."

"Then why are you wasting time chasing down some old dorm instead of filing a formal complaint? He shouldn't be able to get away with this!"

"In a way, I'm glad he shot me down. The real story lies in that building—and I'm going to break it wide open."

"Come again?"

"You heard me," Claire said firmly. "Why else would someone send me that info? It only confirms what I suspected."

The frustration in Bobby's eyes softened into concern. "I can't let you go alone. It's a dangerous hike through the woods. Who knows what's in that building?"

Claire, for all her toughness, knew he was right—and was quietly relieved he was coming.

"Okay, Weatherman. Meet me at the north entrance in an hour, and I'll explain on the way."

"You're welcome," he said dryly. "I'll be there in half an hour. We only have six hours of daylight left—it's gonna get pitch black out there. Bring water."

"Okay, okay!"

"I've been hiking since Scouts. See you in twenty-seven minutes."

*

True to his word, Bobby was already there when Claire arrived—now dressed in full hiking gear, backpack and canteen in tow. Claire, on the other hand, wore jean cutoffs and clutched a single bottle of Aquafina.

He just stared, shook his head, and said, "This way."

As they navigated past gnarled tree trunks and moss-covered stones, Claire filled him in on the missing pieces of her assignment. She dwelled on the silent defendant in the Carl Burton case—why was one student's identity so fiercely protected?

The more she spoke, the more intrigued Bobby became.

"Well," he finally said, "whoever left that envelope is on our side."

"Our side?" Claire questioned.

"Hey—I'm here, aren't I?"

They hiked in silence for another hour until Bobby pointed ahead. A narrow dirt road broke through the trees, leading to a clearing.

"I can see it," he said. "Why the hell would there be a dorm out here?"

"Remember—this was thirty years ago. There was probably a road back then."

"Still," he muttered, "that's a hell of a commute."

*

The building loomed before them. Rusted double doors were

secured with a thick chain and padlock.

"Now how are we supposed to get in?"

Claire pulled out a folded strip of paper. "This came with the map—32 right, 17 left, 19 right."

Click.

The lock popped open, and the chain fell to the ground. A chill crept over Claire as Bobby pushed the doors open.

Inside was dim and musty. Dust choked the air. A thick layer of grime coated the windows, letting in only slivers of light. The student lounge looked like a 70s time capsule—orange sofas, lime green chairs, and psychedelic pillows. A vending machine in the corner still held dusty cans of Dr. Pepper and Mello Yello, with a few long-expired Snack Packs and Twinkies.

They ignored the rickety elevators and headed for the stairwell.

The second floor began with a communal shower. Eight rooms followed, all marked by peeling green paint, rusted bed springs, and moth-eaten drapes. On the third floor, the wallpaper changed—eye-popping pink with giant daffodils and posters of 60s soul groups.

Claire frowned. "Why would a 70s dorm have 60s memorabilia?"
More curious were the signs of life—an open textbook on a desk, a hairbrush, a crusted container of Noxzema. The place looked abandoned in a hurry.

In one room, a corkboard still hung on the wall. A photo of a family. A chore roster, yellowed but legible:

      Glenn Jackson – Trash

Belinda Reigns – Vacuum & Dust
Timothy Granier – Bathrooms
Vernell Johnson – Bathrooms
Bala Agarwal – Night Rounds
Valentina Lopez – Front Desk
Carla Burton – Carpool to Campus

Claire froze. Carla Burton?

Her breath caught. Unbelievable. Daddy's little girl—the seventh, secret whistleblower? What was her privileged ass doing mixed in with common folk?

It felt too convenient.

Suddenly—SLAM.

The sound echoed through the empty hall.

"Bobby?!" she shouted, stepping into the hallway.

No answer. Then she saw him sprinting past the room toward the source of the sound. "Bobby, wait!" she yelled, chasing after him.

He turned into the last room on the right. When she caught up, he was staring at an open closet. But before they could investigate, someone bolted down the stairs.

"Stay here!" Bobby snapped, then tore after the intruder.

"No! Bobby! Wait!"

Too late.

Standing on the threshold, Claire noticed a navy-blue handkerchief at her feet-faded-dust ridden-yet, recognizable. She took out her phone and snapped a picture.

Heart still hammering, she turned back to the closet. Inside was a pile of shredded, stained fabric—bed sheets, maybe. She knelt and picked up a strip with brown discoloration. Another was attached to an elastic waistband, stained yellow.

Realization hit and Claire cried out- flinging the urine-stained panties across the room. Then Bobby returned—gripping a hoodie-clad figure by the arm.

"Get in there, boy!"

Claire's jaw dropped. "What are you doing, Bobby? We're not gangsters!"

Bobby yanked the hood back.

Her stomach dropped.

"You know this douche?" Bobby demanded.

Claire could barely whisper. "Yeah. That's Sam-my Journalism professor."

Chapter 6

The Culprit

"Sam?!" Claire yelled. "What are you doing here?! How do you even know about this place?"

"I've done some digging on my own because I want to make sure you get your facts straight."

"Facts? What facts?! You said my story was garbage! You humiliated me!" "

What you needed was a push in the right direction—and I gave it to you!"

Bobby shoved him in the back. "Like that, asshole? She's not some chess piece you move around!"

"Enough is enough!" Sam flared. Will you tell your friend here to keep his hands off me?!"

"Maybe after you explain yourself!" Claire demanded.

Sam yanked his arm from Bobby's grip-walked over to one of the beds and perched on the deteriorating mattress. He took a deep breath, and gave Claire a look that said, *Watch yourself.* Then he began.

"My reasons are pretty selfish actually... but I suppose it doesn't matter why I'm doing this—because the end will justify the means."

"Quit stalling, Professor; we haven't got much daylight left!" Bobby snapped.

"My father..."

"Dean Janson?" Claire questioned. "What does he have to do with this?"

Before Sam could answer, a voice echoed from the stairwell: "Sammy? What's taking so long? The mosquitoes are eating me alive!"

"Up here!" Sam shouted back.
All eyes turned toward the doorway, unprepared for who was about to walk through.

Claire's heart sank when her eyes met Kat's. For a moment, both were speechless— confused. Sam watched the two of them with a certain resolve, glad the truth was finally coming out. Bobby, on the other hand, was completely clueless, and it showed.

Then, as if things couldn't get any stranger, Kat crossed the room and slipped her hand into Sam's—an unmistakably intimate gesture.

"Whoa! Okay... what exactly is happening right now?" Claire asked.

With a flip of her hair and a look of defiance, Kat gave the most ludicrous explanation.
"Sam and I are together—as a couple."

Claire's jaw dropped and a stunned Bobby blurted out, "I thought you said he was racist!"

"He is—this is ridiculous! And you, Kat, are a fool! No wonder you're having an identity crisis!"

"As hard as this may be for you to understand, Claire, we are in love. And love is color blind."

"Claire's laugh was dry and cold. "That's rich. It wasn't 'color-blind' when you told me to tone down my Blackness."

"Because you always seem like you have something to prove—you're over the top!"

"Really? Well, you're just his temporary, lukewarm piece of dark meat! He will never be with you in public!"

Eerily calm, Sam interrupted Claire's rant. "You sound like my father—who, by the way, is the reason I am handing you this story."

"You're not handing me anything—I worked my ass off!"

"Slow down," Bobby urged. "I'm interested in hearing him out."

The atmosphere exhaled its tension as each person retreated to a corner of the room.

"First, Claire—I may be many things you probably despise, but a liar and a racist aren't among them. Unfortunately, my father and his friends *are* racists, seeking to rid Brunston of all color—including you, Kat, and Bob, here. I do believe there is a list with your names on it. Are you prepared for that?"

"If you have all this information, why don't you handle this mess with your salad-eating self?"

Sam's lips creased into a patient smile. "Because my father and his friends sit on the Board of Academic Affairs. If I out them, they'll label me a disgruntled employee. Remember—Kat is an undergrad, and I'm her professor. We've both broken the code of ethics. To punish me, the Board can and will place me on indefinite leave. Afterward, no university in the country will hire me. Kat would also become a target—disgraced and possibly lose her scholarship. That is their leverage.

But if you "handle" it, they'll never see it coming."

Bobby looked ready to ride at dawn, Claire, however, wavered —half insulted, half unsure.

"Looks like you'll be teaching night school somewhere—because I didn't sign on for this!"

Sam looked her straight in the eyes.
"Grow up, Claire," his tone teetering on the edge of aggression. "Your article was a fluff piece—a waste of time and energy that wouldn't have changed a thing, and you know it. But the fact that you pushed against the grain? That took guts. It proved you could write something people actually care about. That's why I chose you to break this story."

Kat lowered her head and turned away.

It was clear now—Sam had kept her completely in the dark about his catch-a-crook scheme. And choosing Claire over her to break the story? That was an even sharper blow. The qualities she had buried to belong — to fit in, Sam now admired in someone else.

Claire, sensing Kat's pain, felt bad for her. But be that as it may, she couldn't dispute Sam's instincts. The *Nancy Drew* in her wanted to blow this thing wide open. So, she took a seat and decided to hear him out.

"About six weeks ago, my father caught Kat and me in his guest house and threatened to expose our relationship if I didn't end it. We've been sneaking around ever since. Then one day, while walking in the woods, we stumbled on this place—couldn't believe it still existed. After checking it out, we figured it was safe enough to meet here. I bought chains and a padlock to track who came and went. As far as we knew, no one else had found it."

Bobby wrinkled his nose as he looked around the room. "Whoever occupied this dorm back then, left in a hurry."

"Who could blame them?" Sam muttered.

"Good point," Claire said, crossing her arms. "So, that means you know about Carl Burton— and the lawsuit?"

"I do," Sam answered quietly.

Claire stepped closer. "Then tell me—what about the blood on the ripped panties in the closet?"

Bobby and Kat's heads snapped toward Sam.

"Let's proceed in stages, shall we? I'll try to be as concise as possible."

"That would be helpful," Kat muttered.

"The day my father walked in on us; my mother overheard him from the garden—and she was furious. That evening, I heard them arguing. She brought up his past indiscretion with some... jigaboo—no offense."

"None taken," Claire replied coldly.

"My mother," Sam continued, "swore I was simply a chip off the old block. Said our taste for the 'exotic' must be some kind of genetic defect—and she was done tolerating it."

Kat's mouth gaped. All this time, she truly believed that good manners, hard work, and compromise made you equal. But in that moment—suddenly—she wasn't a student or a woman. She was *just* Black. Nothing else. Just Black. The more Sam recounted the conversation, the more disoriented and sick she felt.

"Margaret," my father said in a strained voice. "We agreed to leave that in the past— now here you go again!"

"Don't hand me that, Neil!" she snapped back. "You let those darkies waltz in here with their drug money and buy that girl a white man's education!"

"What did you expect me to do?!" Neil shouted. "The NAACP, the Board of Accreditation, the scholarship committees—they all had their fingers up my ass and their eyes on everything! I was a puppet—and they were pulling the strings!

If we had to let those people in, might as well take a few rich ones too. Carla Burton wasn't some drug dealer's kid—her parents were prominent attorneys, descended from a long line of vignerons."

"Cocaine, cabernet—what difference does it make?! And I told you not to mention your whore's name in my presence!"

Claire, Kat, and Bobby were so stunned, they couldn't close their mouths.

"Ignoring her tirade, my father walked toward her one slow, deliberate step at a time—and wrapped his arms around her. As always, her stiff, unyielding body melted into his, soothed by his assurances that everything was fine and that their son wouldn't repeat his mistakes.

Sam stood up slowly and walked to the window. His gaze dropped to the rusted wrought iron benches lining the weed-choked garden. He lingered there, hands in his pockets, before drawing a breath and continuing.

A few days later, I went to confront my father in his office. He wasn't there, but something urged me to start searching. Maybe it was the investigative reporter in me. I opened every drawer, checked every cabinet, scanned every corner. Then I saw it—a potted palm, brittle and nearly calcified. Something was sticking out of the dry soil. When I brushed it away, I uncovered an airtight bag containing seven files—each one thick with notes.

I knew I'd struck pay dirt. Pardon the pun."

"Inside the very first folder was all the enrollment info on Carla Burton. Originally, she was assigned to the Beth Brunston Dormitory filled with white, wealthy debutantes who loved the camera. Then, there was a so-called overcrowding issue, and she was transferred here with the rest of the minority students."

"Did you know the living conditions were inhumane?! That they weren't even given decent food?" Claire shouted.

"All of that—and more—is detailed in their complaints. Despite the egregious disparities, Carla was moved in right around the time Valentina and Bala were placed on probation. From there, tensions escalated. The group began turning on one another—especially Carla, who was seen as privileged. Everyone assumed her father could help them, but she refused to involve him because the Dean of Students assured her the accommodations were only temporary."

"Who was that lying S.O.B.?!" Bobby demanded.

"As it turns out, Sam confessed, my father was the Dean back then, too."

All three raised their eyebrows.

"Here's where it gets sticky," Sam continued. "Carl Burton finally made an appearance at Brunston because his daughter had been assaulted."

Claire stood. "What do you mean, assaulted?"

"She was found exposed and passed out in that very closet. Her wrists and ankles were bound with ripped bedsheets..."

Sam's voice cut off. He choked on words too painful to say. Kat placed a hand on his shoulder, urging him on.

"...Her panties, ripped and bloodied, were stuffed in her mouth."

At that moment, you could hear a pin drop.

"My father held a private meeting with Carl Burton on how to proceed. Neither of them wanted the incident made public—not for Carla's sake, and certainly not for the university's. Still, Carl demanded justice.

So, my father turned a blind eye while Carl quietly filed a discrimination suit. Each of the seven minority students named in the complaint received a predetermined cash settlement of $100,000. Carla, meanwhile, would continue at Brunston under total anonymity as a whistleblower. All her privileges were quietly restored—and life went on as usual."

"What about the other six students?" Kat asked.

"Some returned. Some took the money and ran."

Claire's expression was a mix of shock and disbelief.

"Her own father sold her dignity for $100,000?! Claire gasped. Sam, we need to know-who raped Carla?!"

Tears streamed down his face as he turned from the window. "Her statement was redacted. I don't know for sure."

"Why did your mother call Carla your father's whore?"

Sam shook his head, "I can only assume, it was because they were having an affair...

Claire rose to her feet with fire in her voice. "I want those files by tomorrow morning—because I'm going to find the hell out."

Chapter 7

Seven Secrets and a Dead Palm Tree

At seven a.m., Sam stood in Claire's doorway holding a box of files and a crumpled bag of bagels. When he extended both to her, she allowed him inside. Moments later, Bobby and Kat appeared. Bobby strolled in like he owned the place—and secretly, Claire liked it.

Kat lingered in the hallway, silently asking for permission to enter. With one unmistakable look, Claire forgave her, absolving all the hurt and animosity between them. The two melted into an embrace, and just like that, they were friends again.

"Grab a pillow, you guys, and cop a squat on the floor. I'll make coffee."

As they formed a circle on the rug, Claire piled the folders in the center. Each of them immediately took one and began scanning its contents.

Kat held her folder closer to her face, eyes wide with disbelief. "It says here that Bala found Carla and called Dean Janson... Why didn't he call the police?"

"Good question," Bobby said. "Especially since Janson was part of the system that abused them."

Claire looked up from her folder. "That might explain why Dr. Agarwal isn't returning my call. I reached out to him a few days ago and—nothing."

Bobby leaned back, thinking. "You said he owns a broadcasting company, right? He's probably just swamped. Try calling him again."

Claire checked her phone. It was after eight. She gave Bobby's suggestion a try.

"Hello—yes—good morning. This is Claire Richardson, a journalism student at Brunston University..."

The others looked up when Claire suddenly stopped talking. Her expression shifted from hopeful to crushed. She ended the call with a simple, "Thank you."

They all stared at her, waiting.

"What gives, Claire?" Sam finally asked. "What did they say?"

"That Dr. Agarwal is not, nor will he ever be, available for an interview from Brunston alumni. Furthermore, he would appreciate no further contact from me under any circumstances."

"Whoa," said Kat. "Somebody's touchy. But don't let it shake you—it just means we're onto something."

"Jimmy in the cafeteria reacted the same way when I asked him about Carla," Claire added. "He shut me down fast."

"I remember him from my childhood," Sam said. "His mother worked in our household."

"You mean she was your maid?" Kat asked pointedly.

"She was more than that. She organized events, handled logistics, everything. Jimmy was always around—cleaning the pool, running errands. My family and the staff relied heavily on them."

"So he probably knows a lot more than he's letting on."

"No doubt," Bobby agreed. "I say we stop dancing around and go straight to the source. Where's your dad now, Sam?"

"He's briefing security for Freshman Orientation. But I'm not sure this is a good idea."

It was already too late. Claire had downed her coffee and was slipping into her shoes.

The four of them headed to the Dean's office, clearly on a mission. Dean Janson's prune-faced receptionist greeted them with a tight frown, her jet-black hair shellacked into a bun so taut it practically lifted her eyebrows. She looked past the others and addressed Sam only.

"Your father is in a meeting. Can I help you with something?"

"No, Alfreda," Sam replied politely. "We'll wait."

"Suit yourself. Conference Room C is free."

As they took seats around the table, Bobby turned to Claire. "I think you should handle this carefully."

"We have the goods on him," Claire said. "He's not in a position to deny anything."

"He still holds our future," Kat said gently.

"And mine," Sam added.

"He held Carla Burton's future too," Claire murmured.

As if on cue, the door swung open, and Dean Janson strode in. He looked immediately displeased.

"Sam, what is the meaning of this? Shouldn't you and your little tribe be in class?"

"Sir, we're here on a serious matter."

The Dean looked at Kat and sighed. "Son, if this is what I think it is, the discussion is closed."

"No, sir," Kat said firmly. "This is about you."

The room fell silent.

"Excuse me, young lady?"

Claire was stunned and also proud of Kat's newfound confidence. "Like my friend said, Dean Janson, this is about your involvement with Carla Burton."

Dean Janson's face flushed crimson-the veins in his neck pulsed. "Alfreda! Call security!" he bellowed.

Sam, nor the students budged. They stood their ground-eyes locked on Janson with quiet defiance.

"We've got your files," Claire announced calmly—the ones buried in the dead palm tree."

The Dean turned his defeated eyes to Sam. "Boy, how could you? Everything I've done was to protect you. And now you've opened a can of snakes you can't control."

"Tell me about those snakes, Dad. Did you rape that poor girl and then help cover it up?"

 "You don't know what you're talking about!"
"Then explain it to me."

"Or what?"

"We'll expose you and Carl Burton's cover-up."

"Carl and I are just a couple of old men now. The one you'll destroy is Carla."

"Stop pretending you care about Ms. Burton!" Bobby shouted.

"Care about her? Hell—I loved that girl, and I still do!"

Sam swallowed hard trying to process his father's words.

Just then, the receptionist appeared at the door, visibly shaken by the shouting. Dean Janson lifted a finger, signaling her to wait.

"Hold my calls—we're going to need a minute."

Chapter 8

In the Dark We're All Black

"Dad—what were you, twenty years her senior?!"

"Eighteen. And you, above everyone else, should understand."

Heavy contemplation fell over Sam, rendering him silent. Kat was twenty-one, he was thirty five.

"But Carla didn't feel the same way, did she?" Claire accused. "That's why you tied her up and forced yourself on her!"

"No. No. No!" Dean Janson bellowed. "Wrong again! Our feelings were mutual. Why do you think she didn't run home to her father after being stashed in that hellhole of a dorm? It's because she was willing to sacrifice everything for what we had!"

"If you loved her so much, why would you let her—and other minority students—live like bums?" Bobby pressed.

"My hands were tied! Faculty was already furious over Affirmative Action' and being forced to open our doors. They feared that the ways of those inner-city folks would rub off on the upper echelon. And then where would we be? Our status would slip. No more open doors to top networks for our grads—nothing!"

"This is ludicrous—and I'm ashamed to call you Father!" Sam shouted.

"Son, unfortunately, this is the real world. And your shit doesn't smell like roses either!"

"Is your indiscretion the reason Mother hates you so much?!"

"No—but it gave her an excuse. A label to pin on this mismatch of a marriage. I'm sorry, son, but your mother is cold and insensitive. She cares more about place settings and garden parties than she ever did for me. It's always been about appearances. Carla, on the other hand—she was authentic. Warm. Genuinely interested in me. I couldn't resist the pull of such sweetness... such kindness. I loved her. And she loved me."

"Unreal," Claire said aloud.

"Then why did you forbid my relationship with Kat?" Sam asked. "We were careful. We weren't hurting anyone. But you crushed it like you do everything else!"

"Because you don't have the resources to protect her! It would only be a matter of time before your mother made one of her calls, and after that, Kat would be lucky to get into a decent city college! Now, if you and your little posse are done with this Spanish Inquisition, I'll be on my way."

Claire stood. "Well, Dean Janson, if you didn't rape Carla Burton, then who did?"

Dean Janson placed his hand on the doorknob, clearly intent on leaving. "Let sleeping dogs lie, shall we?"
Before anyone could respond, the prune-faced receptionist entered, ushering in a pearl-clad woman in a crisp linen suit. Her squinted eyes surveyed the room.

"I apologize, Dean Janson, but with all the ruckus, I thought it best to inform Mrs. Janson."

"Of course you did, Alfreda, " he replied sarcastically. "That will be all—thank you."

Alfreda paused long enough to register her boss's tone,

then scurried out the door.

"Neil," Mrs. Janson began, "what on earth is going on here? And Sam, aren't these your students? Let's dismiss them and talk in private."

She crossed the room and confronted Kat with sharp eye contact. "I'm sure you understand, dear."

To Margaret's surprise, Sam stepped up beside his girlfriend. "No, Mother. Some things are getting resolved today."

"You and your father won't be happy until you've ruined us!" she screeched.

"That's enough, Margaret!"

"Apparently not! The boy's walking in his daddy's footsteps!"

"Mother, I'm not a boy. I'm a man—perfectly capable of choosing my own friends, my own life. You can't bully me like you bully Dad."

"Neil, what have you been feeding our son to make him turn on us like this? Never mind— you don't have the skillset of an influencer! It had to be this jungle-bunny with her *exotic* skills! But she better watch her step!"

"Is that a threat?" Bobby asked calmly. "Would you care to elaborate, Mrs. Janson?"

"He's right, Mom. What are you saying?" Sam pressed.

But there would be no more answers from Margaret Janson. She swept out of the room, her husband close behind.

Soon, the four of them were back in Claire's dorm, combing through files—only to discover the gaps of information outweighed the answers.

For instance, on the night of the assault, all the students—except Carla—were reportedly out for the evening. Only Bala returned and found her bound, bruised, and gagged. Where were the others?

And why did everyone just up and abandon the dorm, leaving behind their personal items? Why were bloody clues—never properly investigated—still sitting in plain sight?

This wasn't just a sloppy, amateur crime scene. It reeked of arrogance.

Make it make sense.

*

Claire awoke just before dawn and glanced around her room. Her friends lay sprawled across the rug and on cushions, sleeping soundly. She tiptoed to the bathroom and checked her phone.

Several missed calls—from Agarwal Broadcasting.

She blinked. That couldn't be right. The number was different from the one she'd been calling. Her fingers hovered, then dialed.

"Meet me now on the campus path, adjacent to the café. Come alone," said the voice on the other end.

Then the line went dead.

Brushing her teeth and lacing her sneakers, Claire wrestled with her gut instinct. Was it smart to go alone? Or should she wake the others?

In the end, her Nancy Drew spirit won out. She crept quietly through the maze of her sleeping friends, slipped out the door, and followed the garden path to meet a stranger.

Chapter 9

The Others

With the sun barely up, the garden path seemed dark and unsure. Claire stayed dead center, grateful the café was just steps ahead. She planned to stop in for a coffee to survey the surroundings—it wouldn't hurt to be seen by a few people either.

Taking a long sip of brew, her eyes swept the perimeter and stopped when she spotted a man seated on a bench, watching her watch him. It quickly became a now-or-never situation, so she started walking in his direction. The closer she got, the more she could see: older guy, late forties-early fifties, gray hat, jeans, and a blue windbreaker.

From this distance, he didn't seem particularly threatening. When they made eye contact, she immediately recognized him from his Facebook photo. It was Dr. Bala Agarwal.

Claire's first inclination was to run. But then she reasoned—why would he lure her into an open area to hurt her?

"Dr. Agarwal, I presume?"

As soon as the words left her mouth, regret followed.

"Look, kid, this isn't some Sherlock Holmes movie. This is my life—and a dozen others you're fooling with. Let sleeping dogs lie!"

"Why does everybody keep saying that? I won't, you know. Not until I get the truth."

"And then what are you gonna do with this so-called truth?"

"Set some souls free—starting with yours. Why did you come here when you said you weren't interested in an interview?"

"Let's just say I got a call from a very concerned individual who wants me to keep my mouth shut. My company is just hanging on with a minimal amount of grants and sponsorships. I can't afford a lawsuit for breaking a gag order. I'm telling you, leave it alone."

"How will things ever change, Dr. Agarwal, if we let all these dogs keep laying down?"

Suddenly, his eyes darted past Claire's shoulder, and panic seized his face. "I thought I told you to come alone!"

Claire turned around, confused, only to see Bobby peering at them from the far side of the café, coffee in hand.

"Dr. Agarwal, wait—I didn't know... Come back!"

She broke into a run to keep up, Bobby at her side, chasing Dr. Agarwal all the way to his car.

"You know," Bobby said, "we'll continue without you. But your name will still be mentioned. Just tell us what you know."

"Get in," Agarwal said flatly.

Bravely, the two obeyed, trusting they'd get what they came for. He drove them ten minutes off campus and parked in a secluded area. Claire felt certain now—he would talk.

"Listen, and listen well. I did not have anything to do with Carla Burton's..." he paused heavily, "...situation. The Dean asked me to keep an eye out for her, since the others were giving her a hard time."

"Others? What others?" Claire asked.

"The other five minority students we lived with. They grew to hate her—said she wasn't black enough, that the establishment planted her to spy on them. Then, there was good ole Daddy Dean Janson, always making sure she had everything she needed. Didn't sit right, especially when the rest of us were taking cold showers and fighting rats.

"One night, in early November, Belinda, Valentina, and Vernell were smoking grass behind the dorm when they heard voices coming from the utility shed. Vernell opened the door— and there was Dean Janson caught in the act with Carla. They were howling so loud the rest of us ran out. The shame of it was, the more he tried to cover Carla, the more exposed he became. Out of decency, I took off my shirt and offered it to her. That move put me in the Dean's good graces. Later he told me he owed me one.

"From there, it just... happened. I became Carla's keeper somehow. Anyway, in exchange for keeping quiet, the others demanded better living conditions. Valentina wanted her probation dropped. Some wanted hush money. The most absurd request was an invitation to the big Holiday Gala hosted by Margaret Janson. There were always photographers and press there—it made national news every year. So, needless to say, Dean Janson was in a tight spot.

"The night of the event, everyone cleaned up real nice and even sprung for a taxi. When we arrived, all eyes were on us. We knew we weren't welcome, but still—we were in."

Claire and Bobby watched as Dr. Agarwal's eyes glazed with tears.

"Carla saw some girls from her old dorm and tried to mingle.

They shunned her in the middle of the foyer. I grabbed her hand, and we moved as a herd toward the buffet. Suddenly, no one else wanted food. When an attendant asked for our invitations, it dawned on us—we were never formally invited. We were crashing one of the biggest parties of the season.

"We escaped to a hallway on the far side of the staircase. We thought no one could hear us as we vented with racial slurs and remarks about the toolshed incident. Valentina even shouted, 'How's it feel to be black, Punta?!'

"That was the breaking point for Carla. She ran out a side exit across the lawn. That's when a woman—Mexican, I think—stepped out of the shadows and told us to come quietly with her into the library. She said she overheard everything and warned that if those lies spread, it wouldn't be good for anyone, especially the Jansons.

But the others pushed back, insisting they had proof. Moments later, we were face-to-face with the Jansons. Margaret's cold, penetrating stare demanded answers. And as the truth began to spill out, Dean Janson just stood there—silent, helpless-like a deer caught in headlights.

When he offered no denial, it was clear: his wife believed us.

The takeaway? Though the players had changed, the game was still the same. And as always—the show had to go on."

"Margaret put on the grand performance of a lifetime. She escorted us through the gala, introduced us to the press, and announced Brunston's cutting-edge partnership with Affirmative Action. She said the school was opening its doors to the less fortunate. How we deserved every opportunity to succeed.

"Can you imagine our humiliation? We were paraded like

prize hogs at a fair! The flashbulbs wouldn't stop. I'd had enough. I left.

"When I reached the dorm, I searched frantically for Carla and found... well, you know the rest.

"The only thing Bala did not mention was the blue silk handkerchief found at the threshold. One of the first things Claire saw when entering Carla's dorm room."

Frustrated, Claire threw her head back. "If everyone was at the Holiday Gala, then who could have dropped this?"

Both Bobby and Bala stared at the photo of the handkerchief on Claire's phone.

"Maybe one of the guys dropped it on their way out," Bobby offered.

"Coming from her room? Why would they be in there? They hated her."

Dr. Agarwal turned the key in the ignition. They took the hint and climbed out. He drove off without a word.

"There's only one way to find out who owns that blue hanky," Claire said. "We have to look at the pictures from the gala before they take them down."

Chapter 10

1978

Claire immediately called Kat to fill her in on what had happened with Bala. The four of them agreed to meet at the library. When they arrived, nerves buzzing, they began pacing the exterior steps, waiting anxiously for the doors to open.

"I can't stay long," Sam said. "I've got a class. But I trust you all will wrap this up today. Claire—sad to say—your grade still depends on it."

Claire blinked, stunned. *Seriously?*

Just then, the lock on the double doors clicked, and a security guard peeked out.

"Professor, is that you?"

"Yes—excuse us—we'll just be a moment!"

Sam was the only one who slowed down to explain as the others charged past, racing for a cubicle to access the archives.

"Brunston Holiday Gala" was hastily typed into the search bar, unleashing a flood of links, images, and news clips. The event dated back to 1945—an era that seemed more glamorous and innocent. Judging by the black-and-white photos, it had once been the crown jewel of social affairs. These days, people barely stopped by on their way to the airport. Claire could only imagine how the decline gnawed at Margaret Janson.

"Type in the year," Bobby insisted.

As soon as Claire entered "1978," voilà—there stood the six.

How had they missed it before? Six minority students surrounded by their lily-white peers. For a moment, they just stared, shaking their heads. At least now, they knew that part of Dr. Agarwal's story was true.

"Now all we need is a blue hanky," said Kat.

Each took a computer, side by side, scanning the 1978 Gala footage.

"BINGO!" Bobby shouted.

"Could you please keep your voices down?" asked the irritated security guard.

"Sorry," they muttered in unison, rushing to Bobby's screen.

"Look—right there, to the left. Dude is holding a blue handkerchief in his right hand, watching the Margaret Janson show!"

Bobby was right. And although the photo was over thirty years old, Claire had seen that man before. She clutched the side of her head in frustration.

"Maybe it's time for a break," Bobby gently suggested.

"No—it's not that. I've seen that guy before... I just can't remember where!"

"It'll come to you," Sam said. "Right now, I've got to get to class."
"Same," said Kat.

"I'm afraid I have to leave too," Bobby added regretfully. "But we'll meet at your place tonight." He kissed Claire on the forehead and left.

Still racking her brain, Claire hit the print button and took a copy of the photo with her.

After class, Claire was trudging back to her dorm in a zombie-like state when her phone buzzed. To her surprise, it was Dean Janson.

"Hello, Ms. Richardson. I hope you don't mind, but I felt compelled to check on you. To let you know—we're not the cold-hearted monsters you think we are."

"Tell that to Kat."

"Look, just do us all a favor and let bygones be bygones."

Claire hung up. She knew they'd touched a nerve.

She pulled the photo from her pocket and stared at it. That curly hair. Those wild, bushy brows. It drove her berserk—until suddenly, everything clicked.

Heart pounding and lungs burning, Claire ran across campus, adrenaline surging. Flinging open the double doors, she barged past a sign reading Employees Only and stood in a doorway, gasping for breath.

"You again? What's the meaning of this intrusion? You're not supposed to be back here!"

Without saying a word, Claire slammed the printed photo onto Jimmy's desk.

Jimmy slowly broke eye contact, looked down at the photo, then up again—visibly confused. "What is this?"

"Proof," Claire said breathlessly. "Proof that you violently raped Carla Burton."

Jimmy reached for the phone, then paused and instead shut the office door. Claire's fear spiked—no one knew where she was.

"I told you to leave this alone," he whispered harshly. "Now, what proof are you talking about?"

"There!" she pointed. "In the photo—you're holding the handkerchief we found at the crime scene!"

Jimmy locked eyes with her, then slowly sat down. What disarmed her most wasn't his composure—but his laughter.

"Who told you this?"

"I have my sources."

"Sources? Let me guess—Bala Agarwal, right?"

Claire was stunned.

"Oh, señorita," Jimmy said. "You don't have to say another word. Your friend must be feeling desperate to pull something like this... and I always had my suspicions, but now, I'm sure."

"What are you talking about?"

"Bala and I were close, once. He was a sensitive soul with a promising future in journalism. Me? Just an errand boy for the Jansons. But since we were both minorities, no one cared that we hung out."

"He used to talk about this one girl—said he'd give up everything for her. I told him no one was worth that. But I saw how he looked at her."

"Her?" Claire asked.

"Don't play dumb, Ms. Investigator. You know who. Bala loved that girl, but she wouldn't give him the time of day. When he found out she was spending time with Neil Janson, he wasn't the same. It was like a light went out."

"And when that terrible night happened...?"

"Several of them scattered. Bala was one of them."

"But why—if he loved her?" asked Claire.

"That kind of love can make a man do crazy things."

"The handkerchief was yours! I saw it in the photo!"

"Wrong again. I was sweating because the Jansons invited me to their fancy party at the last minute. I was told there would be photos- I didn't know how to act-what to say... Bala told me to calm down and handed me his handkerchief. I was holding it when that photo was taken."

Claire felt faint, leaning against the wall for support. She'd been played. Still, she needed to confront Bala. Let him know she knew.

Jimmy saw it in her eyes. "Claire... let it go." That was the last thing she heard as she left.

Wandering aimlessly, Claire found herself at the old dorms. The sun was low, and angry voices echoed from inside.

"What do you mean it's my wife's fault?"

"She—she—she—"

"She what?!"

Claire recognized the first voice as Dean Janson. The

second—Dr. Agarwal.

"I warned you to stay away—all of you. Imagine my surprise when I heard you were back on campus, talking to Claire Richardson. Carla Burton has been through enough!"

"I know," Bala agreed sadly. "I came to fix things. Throw her off the trail." "What trail?

The statute of limitations expired years ago. Go home."
"I will... after I tell you the truth."

Claire crept to a window and spotted the men near the vending machine. Dr. Agarwal began pacing.

"Well, Bala—get on with it!"

"A long time ago, Jimmy and I were friends.

"Jimmy, the cafeteria guy?"

"Yes. But back then, he was your groundskeeper and pool boy."

"Oh-that's right." Dean Janson recalled.

"Sometimes, I would hang around while he worked. But one day, your wife invited me inside."

That caught Dean Janson's attention.

"She smiled a lot. Spoke in a familiar tone that drew me in—but something felt off."

"Bala—what an unusual name," she said. "I've overheard you and Jimmy talk. You seem fond of that girl—Carla, is it? Bring her to lunch sometime. Show her what a real gentleman is."

Seeing the Dean's glare, Bala added, "This was before I knew you were seeing Carla. I thought I had a chance. "But when I escorted Carla to the house, it was like I didn't exist. The two of them talked, laughed, and drank like they knew one another. I didn't care—it felt good just to be around her." She was a light in all that darkness."

Dean Janson nodded slowly. "My instincts tell me my wife knew about Carla and used you to get close to her."

"Maybe that's why she kept encouraging me to pursue Carla... Then, the night of the gala— after Carla ran off—I found her back in the dorm. In the shower. Crying. She didn't know I was there. When she turned around, we kissed. She reached for me. I thought... I thought she wanted me."

Bala's voice cracked. "I let my hands wander. Then she pulled away, disgusted-she started screaming for me to leave. I was ashamed."

Dean Janson moved closer, his voice rising with fury. "What are you saying, you son of a—?"

"I followed her—pleading, apologizing," Bala said, watching the scene replay in his head. Then I smelled liquor. I heard Carla scream. Something struck me from behind. As I faded in and out, I heard male laughter—one voice said, 'Old Lady Janson's gonna get her money's worth tonight.' When I came to, Carla was bound and bruised. That's when I called you. And then... I ran."

Claire watched silently as Dean Janson stormed out, his car roaring away moments later.

When she entered the old dorm, Bala was still there, weeping—so consumed by guilt he barely noticed her.

"I'm sorry I doubted you, Dr. Agarwal," Claire said gently. "But now's not the time to give up. Let's go."

"Go? Where? For what?"

"To make things right. It's the least we can do."

They followed the winding road toward the Janson home. On the way, Claire pulled out her phone and called Bobby.

Creeping up the grassy knoll, they heard the Jansons on the veranda.

"Margaret, I need you to be honest. Did you have anything to do with what happened to Carla Burton?"

"Of course I did." She smiled. "You were never going to end it, and I couldn't compete with young flesh. I knew about her way before you confessed. Sending her to that hell hole was supposed to scare her off. But she loved you—and you loved her. I wasn't about to let your little taste for dark meat ruin my father's legacy."

"Margaret, do you hear yourself?!"

"If she didn't," Claire said, stepping out with Bala beside her, "we sure did."

Margaret spun around, startled. "Who's there?!

Oh my goodness!" she continued. "These dark ones will be the death of us all!" Margaret shrieked. "But don't think there aren't eyes on you too, missy."

"I don't care who's watching, Mrs. Janson," Claire said, stepping forward. "You're going down."

Margaret scoffed. "Dear, don't you realize that soon, you'll crawl back under your little rock, and this university will go on—just like it always has."

To everyone's shock, Dean Janson stepped down from the porch and crossed the lawn to stand beside Claire and Bala.

"She was a good girl, Margaret—whole, full of life," he said quietly. "She left here broken. Because of you."

"Please," Margaret snapped. "She's on national news every night, making a ton of money. Most would consider her unfortunate encounter a small price to pay. She's fine. And if you had kept it in your pants, we wouldn't be here!"

Dean Janson ignored his wife and turned to Claire and Bala.

"Claire, write your story. Tell it all. Tell it well. Bala—the grant to keep your station alive is yours. Thank you for your honesty. Now, if you'll excuse me... I have a long-overdue phone call to make."

Conclusion

Several weeks passed, marked by the swift removal of Margaret and Neil Janson from the Brunston Board of Directors. Both were expected to vacate campus before the new semester began. Criminal conspiracy charges were pending against Margaret Janson and the two journalists who assaulted Carla Burton back in the winter of 1978.

But the most terrifying part was weighing the price of exposing Carla Burton's long buried trauma. Surely, Dean Janson had warned her before the story broke—or so they all hoped.

Claire's phone buzzed, interrupting her thoughts. It was Kat.

"Turn on Channel Seven. Right now!"

Claire fumbled for the remote, and the television screen lit up the dark room. Her mouth fell open.

There she was—Carla Burton.

Older. Dignified. Yet visibly wounded.

She sat across from Tracey Ruderman, one of the most respected names in primetime journalism. The caption along the bottom read:

"Am I My Sister's Keeper?"

Tracey: *"It's been quite a year—you're a busy woman. Thank you for granting us this exclusive interview."*

Carla: *"I can't think of anyone I'd rather sit across from than* you, Tracey. Especially dealing with such a sensitive topic. I admire, respect, and trust you."

Tracey: "Thank you, Carla-Let's get into it, then. A young woman at Brunston University—your alma mater— recently unearthed a long-buried chapter of your life. Her findings exposed and confirmed your violent assault in 1978. How does that make you feel?"

Carla: "Infuriated. Sad. And worst of all—shattered. This young woman reopened wounds from a time I tried desperately to erase. And I'm not happy about it."

Claire watched as tears slid down Carla's face. She wanted to look away—but couldn't.

Tracey: "Then why go public now?"

Carla: "Several reasons. To get ahead of what could easily become a runaway train—both in my life and in my career. To help free women from the burden of silence. And to vindicate those we too often cast aside as casualties simply because their pain makes us uncomfortable."

Tracey: "Those are powerful reasons. But I have to ask—do you feel vindicated?"

Carla: "Honestly? On good days, yes-I'm healing. On bad days, I'm still floored by B.U.'s publication, laying bare the darkest chapter of my life. But I must commend the journalist—Claire Richardson—for how she brought this story to light. Her work wasn't malicious. It had a purpose. And because of her, I now have a platform to turn pain into power."

Claire turned off the television and set down the remote- She slipped on her bonnet, fluffed her pillow, and finally—finally—let herself rest.